A TREASURY OF HOLLY HOBBIE™

CONTENTS

Rand McNally & Company

Chicago • New York • San Francisco

Published by Ottenheimer Publishers, Inc.
Distributed by Rand McNally & Company
Copyright © 1979, 1978 American Greetings Corp.
All Rights Reserved
Printed in the United States of America
ISBN 528-82341-8

ALL THROUGH THE DAY

What time is it? It's 8 a.m.

Breakfast is over and now it's time
To think about what to do.
Remember, no matter what you decide,
The whole day's waiting for you!

What time is it? It's 9 a.m.

The flowers are ready to be picked,
And the garden seems **full** of blooms,
So take some indoors and arrange them well
To brighten up all the rooms.

What time is it? It's 10 a.m.

Gardening is quite hard work, indeed,
Now it's time to rest a bit,
And think a little on what to do next
When you're fresh and ready and fit!

What time is it? It's 11 a.m.

Late in the morning it's time for fun,
To play with all your might—
To run, to jump, to enjoy yourself
    —and work up an appetite!

What time is it? It's 12, noon.

Peanut butter's good for lunch—
So are soup and tuna fish—
Whatever you have, Mother will see
That it's a tasty dish.

What time is it? It's 1 p.m.

Outdoors again—a lovely day—
And the wind's come up just right.
So untangle the cord—then a quick, hard run—
'Cause it's time to fly your kite!

What time is it? It's 2 p.m.

The wind has dropped, your kite is down,
Time for something else you'll like.
And what could be more fun right now
Than taking a ride on your bike!

What time is it? It's 3 p.m.

In the middle of the afternoon,
Why not take a little walk
By yourself, or with a friend
And have a pleasant talk.

What time is it? It's 4 p.m.

The day's been busy and now you're tired
From all your work and play.
So take a nap to freshen up
For the rest of this lovely day!

What time is it? It's 5 p.m.

Mother's busy—she needs some help—
So into the kitchen you go.
Making a pie takes quite a while,
And it **still** has to bake, you know!

What time is it? It's 6 p.m.

Everyone is hungry now
And you're bound to be a winner
'Cause you have worked to help prepare
A very lovely dinner!

What time is it? It's 7 p.m.

Now the time is growing short
For after-dinner play
Your bed is waiting, you've neared the end
Of an extra-special day.

What time is it? It's 8 p.m.

The day is over—it's time to sleep—
But there's one thing left to say—
Be sure to wake up rested,
Tomorrow's another great day!

THROUGH THE YEAR

JANUARY

New Year's resolutions—
     to do just what we should—
It's good to try to keep them,
     and if we could—we would!

FEBRUARY

In February, valentines
     are so much fun to share.
How nice it is to tell someone
     you really, truly care.

MARCH

March is an in-between month
    when wintry winds are high.
But milder days remind us all—
    spring's coming by and by!

SPRING

When spring returns again each year,
    it makes the world brand new—
With blossoms, flowers, and baby things,
    and sunny skies of blue.

APRIL

April is a rainbow month
    of sudden springtime showers,
Bright with golden daffodils
    and lots of pretty flowers.

MAY

May's a month of happy sounds—
    the hum of buzzing bees,
The chirp of little baby birds,
    and the song of a gentle breeze.

JUNE

June's the time for gardening,
    for outside work and play.
It's such a sunny, friendly month,
    we wish that it could stay.

SUMMER

Summer is a lazy time
    for sitting in the shade,
For picnics, going fishing,
    or just sipping lemonade.

JULY

July's a very special month—
   it's when we celebrate
The birthday of our country
   and the things that make it great.

AUGUST

August brings soft, quiet days
   for carefree, summer fun—
For storing up sweet memories
   and lots of summer sun.

SEPTEMBER

September means it's time again
for going off to school.
The days are getting shorter
and the nights are turning cool.

FALL

Autumn paints the pretty leaves
in colors warm and bright.
Brown and red and yellow-gold
make such a lovely sight.

H. HUBBIE

OCTOBER

What to be for Halloween—
a gypsy or a bride?
A witch or scary goblin?
It's not easy to decide!

NOVEMBER

November is Thanksgiving time,
there's such a lot to do—
Now don't forget the turkey
and all the trimmings, too.

DECEMBER

It's hard to think of anything
   but Christmas in December.
There's so much to look forward to—
   and so much to remember.

WINTER

Snowmen, sledding, skating
   are lots and lots of fun.
They make the winter season
   an especially happy one.

ABC's

A is for **a**pples
  which grow on **a** tree
And b**a**ke into pies
  just **a**s ne**a**t **a**s c**a**n be.

Bb

B is for **b**onnets
   that tie with a **b**ow
And high-**b**utton **b**oots
   that were worn long ago.

Cc

C is for candy
 and rich chocolate cake
And cherry-topped cookies
 that folks like to bake.

Dd

D is for doggie,
    a favorite friend,
From his shiny, black nose
    to his tail-wagging end.

Ee

E is for eggs,
    all fresh from the nest.
Fried, boiled or scrambled,
    we'll eat them with zest!

Ff

F is for **f**riends
who are **f**aith**f**ul and true.
Friends can make everything
such **f**un to do.

Gg

G is for **g**arden
        where ve**g**etables **g**row.
We keep down the weeds
        with a rake or a hoe.

Hh

H is for **h**ome,
a warm cozy place,
Where **th**ere's love in your **h**eart
and a smile on your face.

Ii

I **i**s for **i**ce cream,
so yummy to eat,
A soda or sundae's
a favor**i**te treat.

R.HUBBLE

Jj J is for jack-in-the-box,
a quite jolly man,
Who jumps up and out
just as quick as he can.

Kk

K is for kittens,
so fluffy and small.
The tiniest ones
are the nicest of all.

L is for **l**etters
    the carrier brings
Fu**ll** of good news
    and interesting things.

Mm

M is for **m**usic
on the **m**erry-go-round.
It's a **m**agical, **m**arvelous
kind of a sound.

Nn

N is for **n**aps
in a comfortable chair.
If you're tired **en**ough,
you ca**n** **n**ap anywhere!

O is for **o**veralls—
they c**o**ver y**o**ur knees
S**o** y**o**u d**o**n't get scraped
when y**o**u're climbing up trees!

P p

P is for **p**rayers
    for **p**e**op**le you love,
When your hands are **p**ointed
    to heaven above.

Q q

Q is for **q**uilt
    that you keep on your bed.
It's the warm-as-toastiest
    kind of a spread.

Rr

R is for **r**ainbows
that come with the sun
And b**r**ighten the wo**r**ld
when the **r**ainsto**r**m is done.

HOLLY HOBBIE

34

Ss

S is for smiles,
  big ones or small.
They're sure to bring sunshine
  to one and to all.

Tt

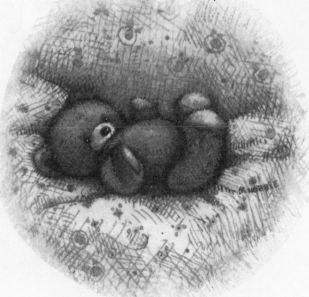

T is for teddy bear—
  a favorite toy—
The number one choice
  of each girl and boy.

Uu

U is for **u**mbrellas
for folks to stand **u**nder
When the skies start to darken
and threaten to th**u**nder.

Vv

V is for **v**ases
  to hold lo**v**ely flowers
Which gi**v**e e**v**eryone pleasure
  for hours and hours.

Ww

W is for **wagon**—
    a s**w**ell **w**ay to ride.
It isn't for indoors
    —only outside!

X is an e**x**cellent
middle or end letter—
It finishes "bo**x**"
and makes "e**x**tra" better.

Y is for **y**arn
for knitting warm mittens
Or rolled in a ball—
for pla**y**ing with kittens.

Zz

Z is for **z**ero.
　　You don't have to be told
That **z**ero is awfully,
　　free**z**ingly cold.

QUESTIONS AND ANSWERS

WHY DO FLOWERS BLOOM IN THE SPRING?

In winter the ground is frozen and dry.
  The seeds use this time for a rest.
But in the spring the ground turns soft and warm,
  and seeds can grow and plants take form
And with flowers we are blessed!

HOW BIG IS THE SUN?

If the sun had nothing in it,
  like a great big hollow ball,
Scientists say a million earths
  wouldn't fill that ball at all!

WHAT IS GRAVITY?

Gravity's the pull
    the earth has on us—
      without it, we'd all float away.
That pull also keeps the moon in the sky
      when night replaces day!

WHY DO PLANTS HAVE LEAVES?

Leaves gather water
    and air
      and sun
    to help our plants grow tall.
So—strong, healthy plants
    couldn't flourish and grow
if they had no leaves at all!

WHAT ARE SHOOTING STARS?

They're chunks
    from things like comets
    that streak across the sky.
We know
    that's how they happen
    but we're still not certain WHY.

WHAT MAKES IT RAIN?

The sun draws water up from earth,
    and clouds form in the sky.
The clouds grow fat and start to drip—
    then the ground is no longer dry.

CAN PEOPLE FLOAT?

In the water you'll float like a duck
  if you fill up your lungs with air.
You'll pop right up and stay on top
  without ever a worry or care!

WHERE DOES SMOKE GO?

Smoke's mostly gases
  from something that's burned,
  and gases are moved by the air.
So that's why the smoke,
  from a candle, let's say,
  mysteriously "goes somewhere!"

45

WHERE DOES SAND COME FROM?

Big rocks break into pebbles,
   then crumble
      into sand.
In particles so tiny
   they can slip
      right through your hand.

DOES EVERYBODY HAVE GERMS?

Yes ... but
If we're careful to keep things clean
   we help chase germs away.
And then we won't be sick in bed
   when we would rather play!

WHAT ARE THE BIGGEST AND OLDEST TREES?

The redwoods of California
    soar hundreds of feet in the sky.
They're the oldest living things on earth—
    they've seen thousands of years go by!

WHERE DO RAINBOWS COME FROM?

Sunshine has colors that we don't see,
    but after a rain, we do.
The tiny droplets catch the sun,
    and *all* those colors shine through!

IT'S A HAPPY DAY

It's time to wake up
    with a stretch and a yawn.
It's morning already—
    the night is all gone.
It's a happy-way,
    time-to-play
        day to have fun.
And there's so much to do
    before this day is done.

The **first** thing,
    the number-**one** fun thing today,
Is to get yourself dressed
    and get ready to play.

Sometimes getting dressed
    can take a long while—
If you like to look
    into the mirror
        and SMILE!
It's a happy-way start
    to a happy-way day
Because it's a
    happy-way game
        that you can play.
Just smile in your mirror
    and see what you'll see
And you'll say,
    "Hey,
        that's **my** smile—
It's smiling at ME!"

The morning's a **good** time,
    a time to explore,
All the world's treasures—
    yes, **that's** what it's for.
It's the best time to get out
    and go for a ride
To see all the pretty things
    happening outside.
You can go by yourself
    or take someone with you.
You'll share oh! such nice things—
    yes, morning's for you!

If your day should be rainy
   that won't stop you—
      oh, no!
Umbrella and boots
   and you're ready to go . . .

But if old Mr. Sun
   is all shiny and bright,
Guess what you can have—
   a picnic, that's right!
'Cause there's just so much fun
   picnic time always brings—
Climbing
   and running
      and swinging on swings,
         and then
            eating all
               of your favorite things.

After your lunch
  you can rest,
    you can talk—
Or read a good book
  or take a long walk!

And then,
   if the afternoon's nice
      and it's hot,
You can do something special
   you'll like a whole lot.

You can go near the water
  and wade or just play
And make it
  an extra-nice,
    fun sunshine day.

And, whenever you want
    there are other things, too.
You can play at your house
    when your picnic is through.
You might sew pretty pictures
    with bright-colored thread
Or take out your paint set
    and paint some instead.

Or if you decide
    playing dolls would be fun
You can dress them
    and feed them
And then,
    when you're done...

54

. . . It will be about time
    to maybe help make
A nice, big,
    for-later, not-now
        chocolate cake
That you'll like a whole lot
    because it will be **yummy**
And make you feel happy
    way down in your tummy!

And when your day's over
    here's what you'll say,
"I had so much fun
    on this happy play day—
A day that was just
    what I knew a day **could** be—
Filled up with fun times
    like a happy day **should** be."

AROUND THE HOUSE

BEING A GOOD COOK

Maybe the cat got most of it,
    when first you started to try.
Now cooking is fun 'cause you're good at it—
    wait 'til daddy tastes that pie!

SEWING

Making a dress for your dollie
    in a pattern that's bright and gay
Is a wonderful way to fill the hours
    on a very-bad-weather day.

TAKING CARE OF POTTED PLANTS

Just give them sun and water
and they'll grow up strong and tall.
And you'll be proud to show them off
when good friends come to call.

KEEPING OUR DISHES CLEAN

When you wash and rinse your dishes,
they're so clean and
shiny too.
And if you've done a real good job,
they'll sparkle
just like new.

PICKING A BOUQUET
FOR THE HOUSE

Houses are happy with lots of flowers—
  the rooms seem to sparkle and gleam.
You'll be glad that you picked them
  and mother will thank you and beam.

GOING SHOPPING

It's fun to go out shopping,
  and it helps
    to make a list.
Then you won't have to worry
  that you'll need
    some things you missed.

KEEPING THINGS NEAT

If you put things where they belong
    and keep them just that way
You'll find them when you need them
    on a busy "cleaning day."

TAKING CARE OF YOUR PET

Your pet needs you to feed it
    and be sure it gets the sun.
But LOVE'S what makes a playful pet
    a healthy, happy one.

TAKING TIME OUT
FOR DANCING

Even grown-up people
    need time-out every day
To do some things they want to do
    and just relax
      and play.

HELPING WITH HOUSEWORK

Sweep, sweep, sweep and dust, dust, dust
    to make the house clean and bright —
It's fun to do things grown-ups do
    if you learn to do them **right.**

STARTING A GARDEN

March winds and April showers
can blow your plants away.
So start your seeds inside the house
and plant outside in May.

KEEPING IN TOUCH
WITH FRIENDS

The telephone helps you keep in touch—
a call can make a friend.
Your chums all love to hear from you,
on that you can depend.